Snake Alley Band

ELIZABETH NYGAARD

ILLUSTRATED BY
BETSY LEWIN

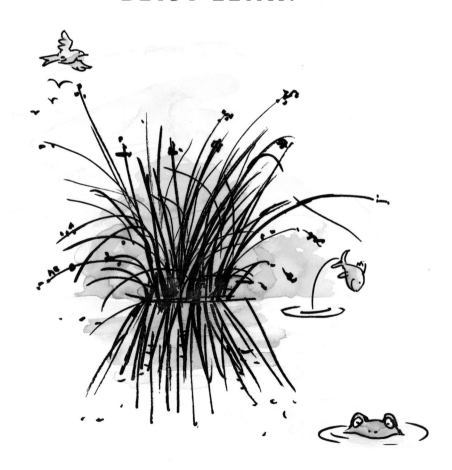

A DOUBLEDAY BOOK FOR YOUNG READERS

At the edge of Fox Woods, not far from Skunk Lane, Raccoon Trail crossed Possum Path. Just a hop away, a skinny point of land stuck out into Lake Minneoko like a snaky tail. Everybody called it Snake Alley.

All the snake bands used to hang around Snake Alley.
In summertime they would slip and slide the night away.
They hissed:
Shhh Shhh Shhh.
They bopped their tails:
BOOM BOOM BOOM.
Shhh-BOOM Shhh-BOOM Shhh-BOOM.

But summer turned to fall and the air got chilly.
One afternoon, the littlest snake tried to keep up
with his band. But he was so tired, his *BOOM*
sounded more like a *plup*.
"You'd better take a nap," whispered his bandleader.
So Snake squirmed into a hole under a log, curled
up, and went to sleep. He slept and slept.

When Old Winter ran an icy finger along the shore of Lake Minneoko, the snake bands hi-de-hoed out of Snake Alley.

Some slipped north along Raccoon Trail to nestle in deserted dens. Some slid south on Possum Path to creep into rocky caves. Somehow in the shuffle, no one remembered the littlest snake sleeping under the log.

All winter long Snake slept, coiled and cozy, his log blanketed with snow.

When spring finally woke him, Snake said, "I'm ready to *Shhh-BOOM*."

So he squeezed out of his hole and slithered off to join his snake band.

He looked high. He looked low.

"Where's my snake band?" he asked.

"Did someone say band?" Cricket popped out of the grass like a jack-in-the-box.

Chew-up chew-up, he chirped.

"I said snake band," said Snake, "not sky-skipping cricket band."

"Did someone say band?" Frog hopped over a log and skidded to a stop.

Cha-BOP cha-BOP cha-BOP, he croaked.

Chew-up chew-up, chirped Cricket.

"I said snake band," said Snake, "not sky-skipping, hip-hopping frog band."

"Did someone say band?" Fish shot out of the lake
and flipped her tail.

POP-POP-DOO-WOP, she bubbled.

Cha-BOP cha-BOP cha-BOP, croaked Frog.

Chew-up chew-up, chirped Cricket.

"I said snake band," sputtered Snake, "not sky-
skipping, hip-hopping, splish-splashing fish band."

"Did someone say band?" Bird twirled like a top, flinging feathers everywhere.

Tweet-tweedle-dee-deet, he twittered.

`POP-POP-DOO-WOP`, bubbled Fish.

Cha-BOP cha-BOP cha-BOP, croaked Frog.

`Chew-up chew-up`, chirped Cricket.

Ah-CHOO, sneezed Snake.

"I said snake band," he said, "not sky-skipping, hip-hopping, splish-splashing, flip-flapping bird band."

"Did someone say band?" Turtle
shook the ground like a passing train.

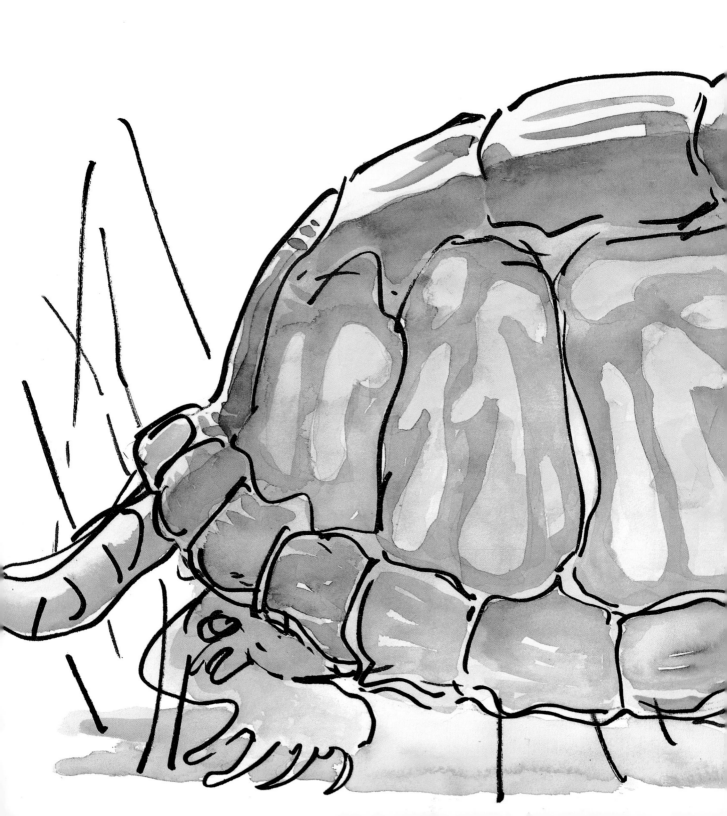

TA-TOOM TA-TOOM TOOM, she thumped.
Tweet-tweedle-dee-deet, twittered Bird.
POP-POP-DOO-WOP, bubbled Fish.
Cha-BOP cha-BOP cha-BOP, croaked Frog.
Chew-up chew-up, chirped Cricket.

SHHH-BOOOM!

"Stop that racket!" shouted Snake. "I said snake
band, not sky-skipping, hip-hopping, splish-splashing,
flip-flapping, stamp-stomping turtle band."

And without looking back, Snake wiggle-waggled away through the grass.

"Band!" He sniffed. "Why, they're just a bunch of noisemakers."

Snake wriggled out of Snake Alley and into Fox Woods.

Way deep in the woods, Snake heard that sweet old sound.

Shhh-BOOM Shhh-BOOM Shhh-BOOM.

He wiggled toward it as fast as he could.

Then by a brushpile, he spotted his old snake band.

The other snakes wagged their tails. "We've missed you," they said.

His bandleader bowed. "Well, bop my tail!" he said. "Let's *Shhh-BOOM*."

All day Snake played with his band.
Then they slipped and slid the night away.
They hissed:
Shhh Shhh Shhh.
They bopped their tails:
BOOM BOOM BOOM.
Shhh-BOOM Shhh-BOOM Shhh-BOOM.
And the music felt just fine.

But the next morning, Snake stopped hissing. He stopped bopping.

"What's wrong?" asked his bandleader.

"All day and all night, our band sounds the same," complained Snake.

"All snake bands sound the same," said another snake.

"Our band could be better," said Snake.

"How?" asked his bandleader.

"There's nothing better than a snake band," said the other snakes.

Snake gulped. "What this band needs is a cricket," he said.

"Say what?" asked his bandleader.

"This band could use some chirping," said Snake. "And a croak here and there wouldn't hurt."

All the snakes hissed. *Ss-shhh Ss-shhh Ss-shhh.*

"You'd better skedaddle," said his bandleader.

So Snake slithered back to Snake Alley.

He said, "Where's the band?"

But all he heard was the whisper of his own tail swishing through the grass.

"Now I've done it," Snake said. "No band wants me."

"Did someone say band?" Cricket skipped over a dandelion.

"I did," said Snake. "I want a sky-skipping, hip-hopping, splish-splashing, flip-flapping, stamp-stomping, wig-wagging Snake Alley band. If it's all right with all of you."

"So right," said Turtle. She tapped: one, two, three, four.
Chew-up chew-up, chirped Cricket.
Cha-BOP cha-BOP cha-BOP, croaked Frog.
POP-POP-DOO-WOP, bubbled Fish.
Tweet-tweedle-dee-deet, twittered Bird.
TA-TOOM TA-TOOM TOOM, thumped Turtle.
"We're the Snake Alley band," they sang as the golden sun set.
Shhh-BOOM Shhh-BOOM Shhh-BOOM!

For Fred, Alex, and Max
—E.N.

A Doubleday Book for Young Readers
Published by
Bantam Doubleday Dell Publishing Group, Inc.
1540 Broadway
New York, New York 10036
Doubleday and the portrayal of an anchor with a dolphin are trademarks of
Bantam Doubleday Dell Publishing Group, Inc.
Text copyright © 1998 by Elizabeth Nygaard
Illustrations copyright © 1998 by Betsy Lewin

Library of Congress Cataloging-in-Publication Data
Nygaard, Elizabeth.
  Snake alley band / Elizabeth Nygaard ; illustrated by Betsy Lewin
    p. cm.
  Summary: When the S*hhh-BOOM, shhh-BOOM, shhh-BOOM* of the snake band begins
to sound a little monotonous, Snake suggests adding Frog's *cha-BOP,* or maybe
Cricket's *chew-up chew-up.*
  ISBN 0-385-32323-9
  [1. Snakes—Fiction. 2. Animals—Fiction. 3. Bands (Music)—Fiction.] I. Lewin, Betsy,
ill. II. Title.
PZ7.N993Sn 1998   97-15544
[E]—dc21   CIP
                                                                          AC
The text of this book is set in 14-point Bookman Medium.
Book design by Trish Parcell Watts
Manufactured in the United States of America
September 1998
10 9 8 7 6 5 4 3 2 1